LADY IN THE WATER

a bedtime story

by M. Night Shyamalan

illustrations by Crash McCreery

LITTLE, BROWN AND COMPANY

New York ~ Boston ~ London

There are ways to know if they are in your backyard.

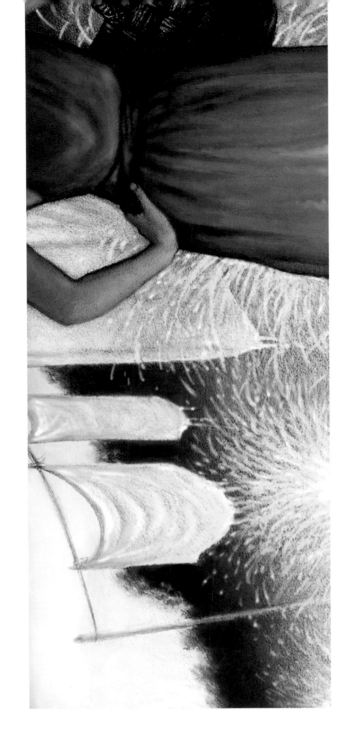

If the sprinklers go off by mistake, you should take notice. It might mean something.

And if you find the water in your swimming pool is a little bit slimy— then it definitely means something.

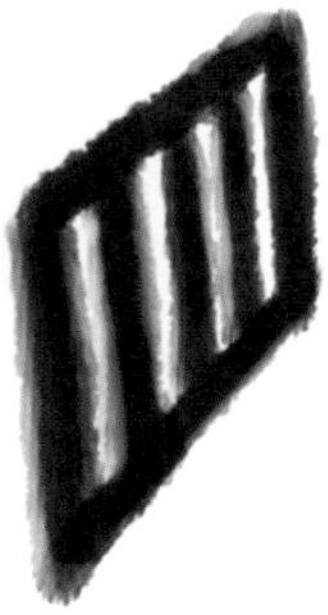

There is someone living
under your pool.
She is called a narf.
She is a very rare type of sea nymph.

She made a room
under your pool after
the pool was made.

She makes a door on the floor of the pool. It is very hard to see. The handle of the door is a small shiny pebble. It glimmers in the sun sometimes and gives itself away. If the grate at the bottom of the pool is big enough, she will use that as the door and save herself some work.

Her room is beautiful. The walls are filled with cracks, thousands of them, like an egg that has been shattered.

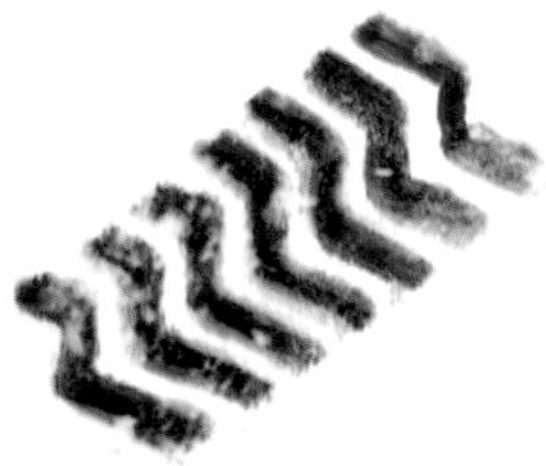

When she leaves, the dirt behind the
walls slowly seeps through the cracks
and collapses the room. That is why no
one ever finds these rooms when pools
are dug up. The rooms are no longer there.....

The only things found will be bits of stone
with scratches on them.
These scratches were words once—
words she and others like her could read.

She lives in
this room for
a short time.
She stays there
during the
daytime.

She is swimming in the pool to be seen by someone in your house. That is her purpose.

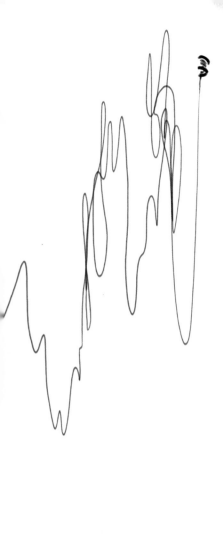

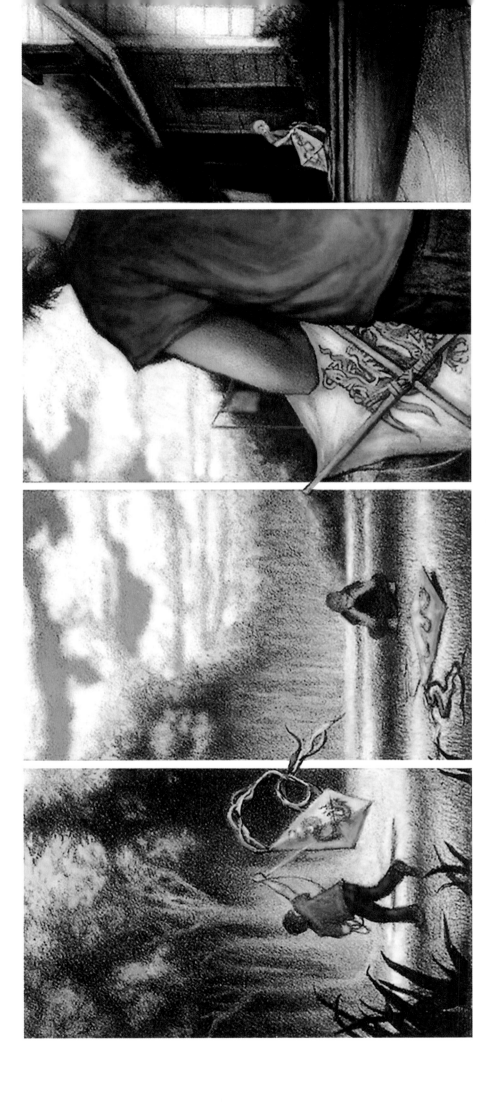

It could be your brother, your sister, one of your parents, or even someone staying at your house for a little while. They will see her only for a moment.

They will look back and she will be under the water. They will think they imagined it... a woman swimming in the dark in the pool.

And then they will feel something happening inside their chest. Somewhere between their heart and their lungs, they will feel pinpricks, like the needles from when we sit too long and our legs fall asleep.

These pinpricks happen because something that was asleep inside these people—something that they didn't even know was there—has awakened.

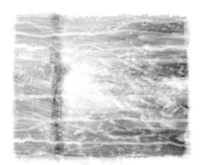

These people are called vessels and they will suddenly feel different. Everything they think will become very clear. If they were scared before, they won't be scared. If they were shy before, they won't be shy.

And here's the best part: sometime in their life—it could be soon, it could be many years from now when they are older—they will do something important for the world.

If the narf is seen by the vessel that lives in your house, she will be taken home that night, back to the ocean, where she will become free.

She will be taken by the last of the giant eagles. He is known as the Great Eatlon, and he is the only one who can take a narf back to the ocean.

Now here's the bad part.

There is someone in your backyard who means to stop her.

He is called a scrunt. He looks like a hyena. He hides in your grass.

The scrunt can lie so flat you cannot see him. His back is covered with grass.

He will look like a bump in your lawn.

He waits for her.

He is allowed to get her if she is out of the water. He has poison in his claws. One scratch will make her feel weak and dizzy. Two will make her very sick. Three scratches...well then, she will die.

There is one night that he is not allowed to touch her—that is the night the Great Eatlon comes. On this night, she is safe.

On this night he can only watch her. He will not break this rule because he is afraid of something.

Tartutic.
They have one name,
but there are three of them.
They look like monkeys.

They are like guards sent
to punish the scrunts
when they break the
rules. They climb down
from the trees and out
of the bushes and snatch
the scrunts away.

All this may be going on in your backyard. There is more to tell of course, like why a scrunt might break the rule and try to attack a narf on the night the great Eatlon comes...because there is a reason.

And there are others to tell about, like there might be someone in your home who can help her if she gets in trouble, but you do not need to know all that right now.

Just keep an eye out for signs of things in your yard.

And one night....

if you happen to glance out your
window and think you see a woman swimming in
your pool....

and then you feel pinpricks in your chest....

know you have just seen a narf and you are her
vessel and one day you will do something important
for the world.

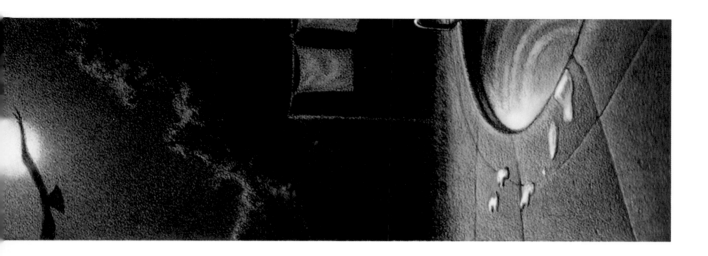

begin

To my cookies,
I love you both.

—Appa

To Dad,
I miss you.

—C.M.

Published by Little, Brown and Company Books for Young Readers
1271 Avenue of the Americas, New York, NY 10020
Visit our Web site at www.lb-kids.com

First Edition: June 2006

Library of Congress Cataloging-in-Publication Data

Shyamalan, M. Night.
Lady in the water / by M. Night Shyamalan ; illustrated by Crash McCreery.— 1st ed.
p. cm.
Summary: Reveals the narf, a rare sea nymph who lives beneath a swimming pool until she is
seen by a person who, after that experience, will someday do something important for the world.
ISBN-13: 978-0-316-01734-3 (hardcover)
ISBN-10: 0-316-01734-5 (hardcover)
[1. Imaginary creatures—Fiction.] I. McCreery, Crash, ill. II. Title.
PZ7.S5622Lad 2006
[Fic]—dc22
2006001390

10 9 8 7 6 5 4 3 2

PHX

Printed in the U.S.A.